Modern Curriculum Press
BEGINNING
TO
READ
Series

The Little Runaway

THE LITTLE RUNAWAY

ISBN 0-8136-5552-8   Hardbound

ISBN 0-8136-5052-6   Paperback   9 10   93

The Little
Runaway

Margaret Hillert

Illustrated by Irv Anderson

MODERN CURRICULUM PRESS
Cleveland · Toronto

Here is a mother.

Here is a little baby.

Come here, little one.

Come here to me.

No, no.

I want to go away.

Here I go.

One, two, three.

Away, away.

It is fun to run away.

Away I go.

I can run.

I can jump.

I can play.

Look up, look up.

Something is up.

Something can go away.

See it go away.

Away, away, away.

I see something.

Something red.

Something yellow.

Down, down, down.

See something come down.

It is fun to play here.

Look up, up, up.

See the little balls.

Little and red.

Oh, oh, oh.

Oh, my.

Oh, my.

It is not funny.

Here is something blue.

I can look down in it.

Help, help!

Oh, oh.

I want to go away.

Work, work, work.

You can work.

I see you work.

Come and play.

We can play.

Up, up, up.

I can not go up.

Oh my, oh my.

Something big.

Big, big, big.

Oh, oh, oh.

Where is my mother?

Help, help.

Mother, Mother, I want you.

I want my mother.

It is not fun to run away.

Here, little one.

Here is Mother.

Come to Mother.

Margaret Hillert, author of several books in the MCP Beginning-To-Read Series, is a writer, poet, and teacher.

The Little Runaway

The story of a runaway kitten, with charming illustrations and a text that uses only 45 preprimer words.

Word List

7	here		two	**16**	the
	is		three		balls
	a	**10**	it	**17**	oh
	mother		fun		my
	little		run		not
	baby	**11**	can		funny
8	come		jump	**18**	blue
	one		play		in
	to	**12**	look	**19**	help
	me		up	**21**	work
9	no		something		you
	I	**13**	see	**22**	and
	want	**14**	red		we
	go		yellow	**24**	big
	away	**15**	down	**25**	where

28